ACKNOWLEDGEMENTS

This book is a special project that could not have been put together without the advice and input from some very admirable people. Because of their support, this book has feelings, too.

Special thanks to . . .

Lee Pepper, Chief Marketing Officer of Foundations Recovery Network, for conceiving the idea of a children's book and supervising the process in its entirety.

Jeff Skillen of SkillSet Enterprises for his shrewd thinking, key assistance in the publishing process and always-relevant advice.

Christopher Salata, a Foundations Recovery Network admissions coordinator and children's book writer who helped inspire and refine the style of the final draft, and who also connected us with our dynamic illustrator, Lily Jones.

Molly Gentry, the tireless FRN graphic designer who laid out this book for publishing.

Beth and her band of young pirates, for their incredible inspiration.

Heroes in Recovery, for persistently carrying the torch for recovery—sharing stories and hosting events across the country in order to break down the paralyzing stigma that keeps people from seeking help for addiction and mental health issues.

The Foundations Recovery Network family; without your passion and dedication to superior service, this book would not have been written. Your infectious hope and desire to see people's lives change for the better inspires us every day.

Printed in the United States of America

First Printing, 2013

ISBN-13: 978-1493674275

ISBN-10: 1493674277

Heroes in Recovery Press

c/o Foundations Recovery Network

5409 Maryland Way, Suite 320

Brentwood, TN 37027

www.HeroesInRecovery.com

Foundations Recovery Network and Heroes in Recovery are registered trademarks

Pirates have feelings, too!

By Anna McKenzie and Kathryn Taylor

Illustrated by Lily Jones

Heroes in Recovery Press

I am a Pirate,
and a great one at that.
Look here,
can you see my bandana
and hat?

I belong to the best Pirate family

My mom,
my dad,
my little sister,
and Me!

And Pirates?
They yell pretty loud sometimes.

Do your mom and dad argue like mine?

Sometimes my dad, he sails far away.

I don't know how long he'll go or he'll stay.

Using my telescope, I search out to sea.

Is he in trouble? Where could he be?

Sometimes I miss him,

sometimes I don't.

Sometimes I'll cry,

and sometimes I won't.

I can be rowdy and I can be tough.
When I go to pirate school,
sometimes I'm rough.

When I get real mad,
I yell at the other kids,

GO WALK THE PLANK AND GET EATEN BY SQUIDS!

Sometimes my tummy hurts, **all topsy turvy.**

Maybe it's crickets— or maybe it's scurvy.

I have so many feelings,
it's hard to keep up!

I put them in my hat,
I stuff and I stuff.

But sometimes my feelings,
they all come out.

ANGRY
SAD
CONFUSED

I just want
to be happy,
not to cry
or to shout.

See all these faces?

I can make them all.

Can you tell to which faces the feelings belong?

Calm   Bored   Confused   Happy

Surprised

Mad   Embarrassed   Scared   Sad

But I'm learning some things
that are important to add.

It's okay to yell,

ARRRRGHHH!

It's okay
to be mad.

I can stomp
my feet by
        myself
again and
        again,

I can let it all out
instead of stuffing it in.

I can hug myself tight
and be brave if I must,

When I sail
to safe places,
I talk to
people I trust.

Yes, being a pirate can be rowdy and rough,

But loving myself and my family's enough.

We all do whatever we can
on the sea

To try to be the best
pirates we can be.

See, now you know. Me? I'm like you.

Believe it or not, Pirates have feelings, too!

THE PURPOSE OF THIS BOOK

This book was written as a resource for kids, parents and therapists to have healthy discussions about family issues, especially addiction and mental health concerns, which can cause considerable strain on the entire family system. We were looking for a way to help children ages 3-6+ express their emotions safely when they are processing the chaos that family issues can bring into their lives. Recovery from substance abuse and mental health conditions is not simply for the individual; all family members must find healing in the recovery process.

We did not desire to paint a rosy picture of recovery, because it is certainly beset with challenges. Each year, approximately 23 million Americans struggle with a substance abuse issue, but only three million actually receive treatment. The mission of Heroes in Recovery is to break the social stigma surrounding addiction and mental health issues in order to pave a path for more people to find healing. While happy endings are not always possible, our goal with this book is to help kids find ways to deal with their pain, conflicting emotions and daily struggles. Learning to talk to "safe" individuals and communicate feelings in a healthy way creates the foundation for inner hope and joy in spite of the circumstances.

You can help break the stigma by sharing your story at HeroesInRecovery.com.

For more information, resources or to help a loved one, please visit us online at FoundationsRecoveryNetwork.com.

ABOUT THE AUTHORS

ANNA MCKENZIE

Anna McKenzie graduated summa cum laude from Ouachita Baptist University with a bachelor's degree in English. She has had the privilege of writing for LifeWay Christian Resources, Worthy Publishing and Foundations Recovery Network, where she is the executive editor in marketing. Anna enjoys being able to combine her passion for writing and editing with the rewarding work of helping people find healing from addiction and mental health conditions.

KATHRYN TAYLOR, MA

Kathryn Taylor holds a master's degree in mental health counseling and a bachelor's degree in public relations and communications. Kathryn specializes in Dual Diagnosis counseling as well as counseling for victims of crime with an emphasis on child, adolescent and women's mental health treatment. She began writing on a freelance basis in 1999 and delights in combining communications and counseling in ways that can enrich others.

My name is _____

My feelings...

_____

_____

_____

_____

_____

_____

_____

_____

_____

_____

My feelings...

_____

_____

_____

_____

_____

_____

_____

When I feel bad, these are the people I can talk to:

_____

_____

_____

Pirate coloring page

I AM A
PIRATE,
AND A
GREAT
ONE
AT
THAT.

My drawings...

Made in the USA
San Bernardino, CA
28 June 2014